MR. QUIET

by Roger Hargreaves

EGMONT WORLD LIMITED.

Mr Quiet liked the quiet life.

He lived, quietly, in a small little cottage in the middle of a wood.

The problem was, that small little cottage was in the middle of a wood in the middle of a country called Loudland!

Everything and everybody in Loudland was noisy.

Oh, the noise!

Dogs didn't go "woof" like dogs you know.

They went (take a deep breath) "WOOF!"

People didn't shut their doors like you or I would shut our doors.

They slammed them.

BANG!

People didn't talk to each other.

They shouted at each other.

"HELLO," they'd shout as they met in the street.

And, you've heard about something being as quiet as a mouse, haven't you?

Not in Loudland.

They had the noisiest mice in the world.

"SQUEAK! SQUEAK!" they'd roar at each other.

Mr Noisy would have liked living in Loudland.

He'd have loved it.

But Mr Quiet didn't.

Noise frightened him.

So, he stayed in his cottage in the middle of his wood as much as he could.

But of course he couldn't stay there all the time.

Every week, for instance, he had to go shopping.

He used to creep into the grocer's shop.

"GOOD MORNING," bellowed the grocer.
"WHAT CAN I DO FOR YOU?"

"Please," whispered Mr Quiet, "could I have some cornflakes please?"

"WHAT?"

"Cornflakes. Please," he whispered.

"SPEAK UP!"

Mr Quiet tried his loudest whisper.

"Cornflakes."

"CAN'T HEAR YOU," shouted the grocer. "NEXT PLEASE!"

And poor Mr Quiet had to creep away without any cornflakes.

It wasn't fair, was it?

He crept into the butcher's.

"Please," he whispered, "I'd like some meat."

The butcher didn't even hear him.

He was humming to himself, loudly and fiercely.

Mr Quiet tried again.

"Please," he whispered, "I'd like some meat."

The butcher started to whistle.

It sounded more like a burglar alarm than a whistle.

Mr Quiet fled.

Empty handed.

It often happened, which probably explains why he was so little.

Poor Mr Quiet.

He sat at home that night with a feeling of despair.

"Whatever am I to do?" he thought.

"It's no use," he thought, "I'll just have to try again."

And so, the following day, he went shopping again.

But, the same thing happened.

"CAN'T HEAR YOU," thundered the grocer. "NEXT PLEASE!"

"CAN'T HEAR YOU," bellowed the greengrocer. "NEXT PLEASE!"

"CAN'T HEAR YOU," roared the milkman. "NEXT PLEASE!"

"CAN'T HEAR YOU," boomed the butcher. "NEXT PLEASE!"

Oh dear!

Poor Mr Quiet went home and went to bed.

Hungry.

The morning after he was awakened by a noise which sounded like bombs dropping.

It was the Loudland postman knocking at Mr Quiet's door.

BANG! BANG! BANG! BANG!

Mr Quiet went and opened the door.

"MORNING," shouted the postman. "LETTER FOR YOU!"

Mr Quiet took the letter into his kitchen.

He sat down to open it.

He waited until the noise of the postman's footsteps died away.

CLUMP CLUMP CLUMP CLUMP clump clump.

Mr Quiet opened the letter in great excitement.

He'd never had a letter before.

It was from Mr Happy in Happyland.

An invitation!

To stay!

Mr Quiet was overjoyed.

He rushed upstairs and packed his bag and set off that very morning.

It was late when he arrived on Mr Happy's doorstep.

He knocked on Mr Happy's door.

Tap tap tap.

Mr Happy opened the door.

"Hello," he smiled. "I thought I heard something. You must be Mr Quiet. Well, don't just stand there, come in and have some supper."

It was the first proper meal Mr Quiet had had for months. And while he was eating it he told Mr Happy all about the problems he'd been having in Loudland.

Mr Happy was most sympathetic.

Over breakfast the following morning, Mr Happy told Mr Quiet that he'd been thinking about his problem.

"I think," he said, "that under the circumstances you'd better stay here in Happyland."

Mr Quiet's face lit up.

"And," continued Mr Happy, "we'll find you a house, and," he went on, "a job."

Mr Quiet's face dropped.

"I'm not very good at jobs," he confessed, "because I'm too quiet."

"Ah," smiled Mr Happy. "I have the very job for a quiet chap like you!"

And so, the very next day, Mr Quiet started work.

And he loves it.

Do you know where he works?

In the Happy Lending Library!

As you know, everybody who goes into a library has to be very quiet, and only whispering is allowed.

What a clever idea of Mr Happy's, wasn't it?

And these days, Mr Quiet is as happy as can be.

Why, only the other day, do you know what he did on his way home from work?

He was so happy he laughed out loud.

Can you imagine?

Tee hee hee!

"NEXT PLEASE!"

·RETURN THIS WHOLE PAGE·

3 Great Offers For Mr Men Fans

1 Token
EGMONT WORLD

1 FREE Door Hangers and Posters

In every Mr Men and Little Miss Book like this one you will find a special token. Collect 6 and we will send you either a brilliant Mr. Men or Little Miss poster and a Mr Men or Little Miss double sided, full colour, bedroom door hanger. Apply using the coupon overleaf, enclosing six tokens and a 50p coin for your choice of two items.

Egmont World tokens can be used towards any other Egmont World / World International token scheme promotions., in early learning and story / activity books.

Posters: Tick your preferred choice of either Mr Men ☐ or Little Miss ☐

Door Hangers: Choose from: Mr. Nosey & Mr Muddle ☐, Mr Greedy & Mr Lazy ☐, Mr Tickle & Mr Grumpy ☐, Mr Slow & Mr Busy ☐, Mr Messy & Mr Quiet ☐, Mr Perfect & Mr Forgetful ☐, Little Miss Fun & Little Miss Late ☐, Little Miss Helpful & Little Miss Tidy ☐, Little Miss Busy & Little Miss Brainy ☐, Little Miss Star & Little Miss Fun ☐. (Please tick)

ENTRANCE FEE 3 SAUSAGES

MR. GREEDY

2 Mr Men Library Boxes

Keep your growing collection of Mr Men and Little Miss books in these superb library boxes. With an integral carrying handle and stay-closed fastener, these full colour, plastic boxes are fantastic. They are just £5.49 each including postage. Order overleaf.

3 Join The Club

To join the fantastic Mr Men & Little Miss Club, check out the page overleaf NOW!

· RETURN THIS WHOLE PAGE ·

Join Our Club!

MR. MEN & Little Miss CLUB

When you become a member of the fantastic Mr Men and Little Miss Club you'll receive a personal letter from Mr Happy and Little Miss Giggles, a club badge with your name, and a superb Welcome Pack (pictured below right).

You'll also get birthday and Christmas cards from the Mr Men and Little Misses, 2 newsletters crammed with special offers, privileges and news, and a copy of the 12 page Mr Men catalogue which includes great party ideas.

If it were on sale in the shops, the Welcome Pack alone might cost around £13. But a year's membership is just £9.99 (plus 73p postage) with a 14 day money-back guarantee if you are not delighted!

HOW TO APPLY To apply for any of these three great offers, ask an adult to complete the coupon below and send it with appropriate payment and tokens (where required) to: Mr Men Offers, PO Box 7, Manchester M19 2HD. Credit card orders for Club membership ONLY by telephone, please call: 01403 242727.

To be completed by an adult

❑ 1. Please send a poster and door hanger as selected overleaf. I enclose six tokens and a 50p coin for post (coin not required if you are also taking up 2. or 3. below).

❑ 2. Please send __ Mr Men Library case(s) and __ Little Miss Library case(s) at £5.49 each.

❑ 3. Please enrol the following in the Mr Men & Little Miss Club at £10.72 (inc postage)

Fan's Name:_____Fan's Address:_____

_____Post Code:_____Date of birth:___/___/___

Your Name:_____Your Address:_____

_____

Post Code:_____Name of parent or guardian (if not you):_____

Total amount due: £_____ (£5.49 per Library Case, £10.72 per Club membership)

❑ I enclose a cheque or postal order payable to Egmont World Limited.

❑ Please charge my MasterCard / Visa account.

Card number: | | | | | | | | | | | | | | | | |

Expiry Date: ____/____   Signature: _____

Data Protection: If you do **not** wish to receive other family offers from us or companies we recommend, please tick this box ❑. Offer applies to UK only